11/8/13

To Henri Enjoy the
Book

```
█ ║█║ ║█║║║ ║█║║║█║ ║█║║║█║ █
D1560105
```

Conrad F.

For the young
who see without limits in
this world... Explore YOUR
imagination!

Caught in a massive Texas pelting of rain, lightning and destruction, Rocky is lost! His siblings Roxy and Rexy believe…Now, this must surely be the end for Rocky! However, for Rocky Raccoon, he can't imagine anything but another beginning.

Rocky must now face his own personal magical adventure filled with fun, mystery and doom. With the speed of a mountain cat and the agility of a Texas rattlesnake, Rocky fights off pirates, monsters, and terrible things that hunt him in the night. Then without warning, Rocky loses his grip on his only hope to survive!

Found starving and lost in the Big City, Rocky's new bronco riding sidekick, Buff, guides them through an adventure that must surely be their end! At last, Rocky believes they have gone through the worst things imaginable. …

Then they meet up with Fang and his sister Evila, a gruesome twosome determined to make Rocky and Buff their lunch menu.

Can these two loyal friends vanquish their foes after all they have gone through?

Will it most certainly be the end?

DOOM! LAUGHTER… ADVENTURE…

THE FIGHT

FOR

FANG!

by

Cameron & Michael Ferweda

Zinger Digital Media

Visit us at www.RockyRaccoonKids.com

Library of Congress Cataloging-in-Publication Data
Ferweda, Cameron and Michael
The Fight For FANG / by Cameron and Michael Ferweda;
Illustrations by Jeanine Henning
p. cm.- (The Great Adventures of Rocky Raccoon; bk 1)
Summary: Rocky is lost in a terrible storm when he comes face to face with his worst nightmare, Fang! Can Rocky and his friends vanquish this foe?
ISBN 978-0-9910150-0-9 Paperbound ((LIB. BDG.)
[1.Story Tales, Folk Tales, and Myths-Juvenile Fiction 2. Raccoon-Juvenile Fiction 3. Action & Adventure-Fiction 4. Comic and Humor-Young Adult Fiction 5. Magic-Young Adult Fiction 6. Rocky Raccoon-Fiction 7. Fang-Fiction 8. Fantasy-Fiction]

Printed in the United States of America, October 2013
McCarthy Print, Austin Texas

Zinger Hardware is a registered trademark

For Katherine,

who always believes in her men

and their magic!

CONTENTS

PROLOGUE: A MOMENT IN TIME 1

PART 1: DON'T STRAY FROM HOME
    CHAPTER 1: ONCE UPON A TIME. 6
    CHAPTER 2: CHATTY CATHY 8

PART 2: A STORM OF ALL TIME!
    CHAPTER 3: CAPTAIN HOOK. 16
    CHAPTER 4: BIG KAHUNA. 19
    CHAPTER 5: IT'S A MONSTER! 22
    CHAPTER 6: AN OLYMPIC GOLD. 25
    CHAPTER 7: THE ROCK 28
    CHAPTER 8: A HORRIBLE THING. 31

PART 3: THE BIG CITY
    CHAPTER 9: IT'S MAGIC. 36
    CHAPTER 10: RETREAT! 39
    CHAPTER 11: WALLY'S HAMBURGERS 43

PART 4: DOOMED!
    CHAPTER 12: MEET FANG & EVILA 48
    CHAPTER 14: UNCLE PAULIE. 55
    CHAPTER 15: BUFFARINO ("BIG FROG") 58
    CHAPTER 16: LUNCH MENU. 62

PART 5: KEEP YOUR WITS!
    CHAPTER 17: THE LAUGHING SCENE. 68
    CHAPTER 18: A FULL HOUSE 71
    CHAPTER 19: REUNION STATION 74
    CHAPTER 20: THE END 77

EPILOGUE: IS IT THE END?. 79

THE GREAT ADVENTURES OF ROCKY RACCOON

THE FIGHT FOR FANG!

PROLOGUE

A MOMENT IN TIME

My son, Cameron, and I live in Austin, Texas and want to tell you a fantastical story.

Our story is about a very special raccoon who survives a terrible storm. This thunderstorm was no ordinary boom, rattle, and shake T-storm. Instead, this was a massive Texas pelting of rain, lightning strikes, and destruction. Every square inch of the city was tested. For if, there was a loose shingle, window, or board, it surely tore free in the storm's fury. I tossed and turned with the thought of what might happen in such a storm if one did not have shelter.

THE GREAT ADVENTURES OF ROCKY RACCOON

5:30 a.m., I felt the last of the thunderstorm's strength give out and the sun began to break through the morning clouds. Our family was deeply concerned by the possible damage done to our store, Zinger Hardware, during the night. I dressed frantically and drove with the hope our store was not destroyed.

Thankfully, upon arriving at the store, I found everything to be normal with only one exception. All-over the front window from my waist down was dripping mud. How strange this was for the nearest grass, bush, or anything remotely living was 300 feet away.

I could not ascertain how or why this mud would be all over the front windows. I kept scratching my head pondering, "Could it be a child finger painted the storefront windows with mud? We just had one of the worst storms in Texas history. Why wasn't the mud washed away? Where did the mud come from?"

Scratching my head, I kept thinking. With a parking lot this huge and no grass or dirt for 300 feet, where could the dirt have come from?

Dumbfounded, I walked along the building wondering how this could happen... ? Just as I turned the key to the side entrance, I found a small raccoon shivering in the corner of the building.

THE FIGHT FOR FANG!

Ah, it was an exact moment in time. A minute later and I would never have known who made the dripping muddy mess on our storefront windows.

Now I know the rest of the story. This little guy had been lost in the storm. Seeing the lights on in the store the raccoon, merely a kit, instantly must have thought he had found the perfect place to hide. To his dismay, the glass prevented him the refuge of the store. The young raccoon had spent the night pawing at the windows to get in.

I immediately started calling shelters to assist with a rescue.

Now, before I could find an animal shelter open, something terribly wrong happened. I heard a loud noise that sounded like a small rocket firing into the air.

Running to the side entrance, I watched in dismay as the landscape crew arrived with leaf blowers blazing. The supervisor of the crew began wildly chasing the small raccoon across the expansive parking lot and into the only tree left in our bleak, desolate, commercial shopping center. The shopping center, neglected for many years, took on an eerie feeling in the morning light. Like most shopping centers that have been left to perish, there remain very few plants... less one solitary tree!

THE GREAT ADVENTURES OF ROCKY RACCOON

My heart sank for the little raccoon. I knew he must miss his family. The raccoon was now all alone in the big city, with no one to give him shelter.

That evening I told this story to my son, Cameron. He decided this certainly must not be the end of the kit's story.

This is the young raccoon's story.

THE FIGHT FOR FANG!

PART 1
DON'T STRAY FROM HOME

CHAPTER 1

ONCE UPON A TIME...

*O*nce upon a time, there are three mischievous little raccoons living with their Ma near the Missouri Pacific railway tracks. The railway, better known as MOPAC, is one of the oldest railways west of the Mississippi River.

THE FIGHT FOR FANG!

Now keep in mind little raccoons are called "kits".

These little kits names are:

Rocky Raccoon, the youngest and the most imaginative

Roxy Raccoon, the second oldest and the sensible one

Rexy Raccoon, the eldest and the protector of the family

I WONDER HOW MA CAME UP WITH THEIR NAMES!

CHAPTER 2

CHATTY CATHY

*L*et's begin!

"Rocky! Are you ever going to stop playing that DS game you found at the picnic grounds? I need you to help clean up this mess."

"Rexy! Stop licking yourself."

Rexy looks up, with embarrassment. Raccoons do preen themselves, but Rexy is out of control. His fur is so slick he looks like the rock star in the crumpled Rolling Stone magazine used as bedding for the kits.

THE FIGHT FOR FANG!

Roxy, feeling the need to support her mother, pipes up in her best hipster voice, "Yeah, Hello! Definitely not appropriate in this house."

Their mother continues chattering as the boys make faces pretending to be Ma without her seeing them. Rexy and Rocky begin to dance in rhythm to her chattering. Rocky attempts to imitate the moon walk while Rexy spins wildly on his back waving his hands in and out like a beetle in distress.

Ma continues chattering at the boys. "And Rexy, I do not want to hear any more wild ideas of you going into the Big City. Do you hear what I am saying?"

Rexy and Rocky stop their shenanigans and look out over the beautiful Texas Hill Country. Rocky nudges Rexy and lets out a "Wow!" From their den, the two raccoons can see in the distance a fantastic display of glittering colors and bubbling lights. It appears the Big City of Austin is a treasure chest waiting for discovery.

Rexy turns back towards his mother. She continues chattering. "Your Uncle Paulie went into the Big City and we have never heard from him again. And you know what happened to your father?"

It seems that Ma can't stop chattering and chattering. I suppose this is why they call her Chatty Cathy. "Remember kits, do not wander too far off. You know what happens to kits that wander too far off!"

"OOOOH." Rexy stands up, hunkers over, and walks like a monster. He stares straight at his sister and in a raspy voice, imitates his mother. "No one ever returns from the Big Evil City!" Rexy lets out a hauntingly scary laugh. "Haa Haa Haa, Hherrr."

Roxy whispers back to Rexy, "With Ma chattering like that, who wants to return from the Big City?" With Ma still chattering, Rexy suggests they all sneak out into the forest, along the train tracks, to play.

The three kits begin to chuckle as they continue listening to Ma. "Remember Aunt May? She wandered off with that young kit. Remember that … Roxy? Rexy! Rocky… yyy!"

Ma continues chattering while the three kits slip off to play. All Rocky, Roxy and Rexy want to do is play and play and play. You know how moms are. Particularly Ma! Chatty Cathy was never going to let up with the scary stories about the Big City.

Their decision to go out that evening will nevertheless change everything for the three kits!

They all have ideas of games to play as they make their escape. *This is going to be the best evening of all time*, Rocky says to himself.

"We are going to have the bestest night of all time!" he shouts.

THE FIGHT FOR FANG!

The three kits are having so much fun they don't realize its past dinnertime. The fun continues until a few tummies begin to rumble. Rocky yells to the others, "Let's look for some blackberries!"

"Or maybe raspberries?" Roxy adds. "Maybe we can get lucky and find some juicy grapes on one of the ranches along the creek."

"Yes, let's go off to the creek," Rexy exclaims.

Now on this particular evening the three raccoons find exactly what they want. Nestled some distance from the train tracks lies the creek. It will be well worth the venture, thinks Rocky.

To get to the berries they just have to cross the creek at a point where an old tree had fallen. "It's Show Time," Rexy shouts as he runs across the log to the other side. Rexy is right, once across the log its dinnertime, Rocky thinks. Everything will be fine.

The far bank of the creek abounds with so many Texas blackberries the three kits forget all about the time as they eat and eat. Their bellies protrude as they lie on the ground like over inflated pool pals. In fact, Rexy looks like a stuffed Barney with berry stains all over himself.

They continue lying around and giggling about everything their Ma has ever said. Tickled with so much chattering, they begin to laugh harder and harder.

They even think for a moment they are becoming their Ma, chatterboxes, Chatty Cathy chatterboxes. And chatterboxes they are!

"Chatter, chatter, and chatter!" Rexy yells rolling about with laughter. Rocky has not had this much fun,

THE FIGHT FOR FANG!

ever. In fact, he tries to cross his legs to not accidentally pee from so much laughter. The fun goes on for what seems to be hours.

Until Rexy, the oldest, notices it's getting light!

THE GREAT ADVENTURES OF ROCKY RACCOON

PART 2
A STORM OF ALL TIME!

CHAPTER 3

CAPTAIN HOOK

*R*oxy, the most sensible, notices her brother's concern. She reminds the others, "Ma will be furious if we don't get home soon."

She will never stop chattering about us being out so late without an adult, Roxy worries.

"She is going to think we went to the Big City never to return," Rexy jokes. Laughing and giggling they continue. So it goes as the three kits head home. The three bandits run in circles, tumbling and tussling along the return path to their home.

THE FIGHT FOR FANG!

Just as they begin to approach the creek crossing, at the old log, the sky turns black as the ink from a skunk. The lightning screeches and the wind howls like the coyotes. Rocky is afraid to cross the creek. He fears crossing even though the three kits have crossed the log many times before. He can barely see the log in front of them as they approach the water's edge.

Rexy, the bravest and the oldest, goes first, in order to guide the other kits across. Rocky shivers, for his brother looks very ghoulish when the lightning flashes and the shadows cast that eerie glow everywhere.

Roxy is next, and she almost crosses the log when Rocky begins to imagine Captain Hook yelling to him. He can see him, standing on the creek's bank, shouting to him, "Walk the plank. Walk the plank, matey, or else."

Rocky imagines being on Hook's pirate ship and having the mean old Captain force him to "Walk the plank!"

The storm sounds like the sailors chanting, "Walk, Walk, Walk, Walk." So nervous about being stranded on the other side, Rocky quickly jumps onto the log and begins to run.

A bolt of lightning strikes the tree on the opposite bank just when Roxy reaches her brother, Rexy.

KAAWACK!

The lightning strikes only a few feet behind Rocky. Before any of the kits know what's happening, a large branch crashes onto the log. The force of the branch causes the log beneath Rocky to collapse. Roxy yells out for her little brother, but he can't keep his balance.

Rocky falls from the log and grabs ahold of a small flat piece of wood that has fallen from the stricken tree.

Roxy and Rexy think, *Now this must surely be the end for Rocky*.

However, for Rocky, he can't imagine anything but another beginning.

CHAPTER 4

THE BIG KAHUNA

*T*o Rocky, the piece of wood feels like a surfboard. He can use it to **ride the wave** down the creek. "Hey Dude check it out," he yells to his brother.

Rocky searches for his sister. He only catches glimpses of her as the lightning lights up the sky. In minutes, he can no longer see either Roxy or Rexy and the rain fully covers his eyes.

Now, Rocky is unsure if he should be scared or just plain excited. So he hangs low on his board and tries to hold on as he pretends to be a great surfer from the North Shore of Hawaii. Rocky imagines being the Big Kahuna and surfing the wave. He surfs through **the tube**.

Rocky hears the crowds cheering for the Big Kahuna as he attempts to do a double flip on his mighty surfboard. Rocky rides the wave in and out of the tube. He runs the whole length of the wave feeling victorious. He decides to showoff for the crowd.

THE FIGHT FOR FANG!

The crowd roars as Rocky inverts in the wave and completes an impressive corkscrew out of the tube. Rocky lands riding with only one hand on the surfboard.

CRACK!

The lightning smacks the creek bank immediately next to Rocky. In that flash, he realizes there are no crowds, no great surfing contests, and no place to ride the great waves of the Hawaiian North Shore. The Texas sized thunderstorm makes him realize, he really wants to be in Hawaii at that moment.

After all, it would be a much safer place than this creek.

CHAPTER 5

IT'S A MONSTER!

*W*ithout warning, the creek's water begins to run faster and faster.

In fact, the creek runs so fast Rocky can no longer think about grabbing onto the riverbank. All he can do is ride the wave and bank his board. He must surf around an awful lot of debris and odd looming objects. He skims an ice chest, slides over a Big Wheel, and shoots off a doghouse roof. At first Rocky thinks, *the ride is fun and exciting*. Now he realizes *this adventure is taking me too far from home. And I am a little bit scared*…you don't say.

Shadows begin to look more like monsters, and Rocky begins to see things on the riverbank. Huge creatures loom above him and they appear to have glowing eyes.

THE FIGHT FOR FANG!

The wind turns almost thunderous, and he starts to think *this may not be the bestest night after all*.

Then, suddenly, in front of him, something large and strange materializes in the middle of the creek.

IT'S A MONSTER!

The water flies from the monster's face and sprays everything within fifteen feet. Rocky sees fire shooting from the depths of the creek upward in his direction. He **Ziggs**. He **Zaggs**. But no... *the creek's current is too strong!*

Oh no! No, no, no! Rocky realizes he is heading straight for the monster's flaming mouth, and the fire blinds him.

Rocky holds his breath for he knows *this is definitely the end*. He heads straight into the monster's mouth and *I am going to... be... eaten!*

He hears sounds of metal and iron, and raging water covers Rocky.

But nothing happens!

Rocky realizes the monster is only a jeep with its headlights blazing that ran off the road and into the creek during the storm. He rode through the open windshield and out the back door. The half-hung door offers Rocky a ramp to jump and he yells out "YAHOOO" as he fends off the monster.

"Take that!" Rocky yells, as he does a little dance on his awesome surfboard.

CHAPTER 6

AN OLYMPIC GOLD

*R*ocky soaks in the thrill of defeating the monster and does not realize the creek begins flowing at an even faster pace. Now supersonic the creek rushes downward to an unknown end.

Suddenly, without warning, the creek starts spiraling. Rocky quickly moves forward onto the surfboard as the creek narrows and rushes even more steeply downward. The creek's banks are now concrete barriers that slowly force the water to go beyond supersonic. Rocky's speed accelerates to hyper-speed!

Rocky thinks, *Hello, this definitely is the end!*

THE GREAT ADVENTURES OF ROCKY RACCOON

Rocky does his best to stay on his makeshift surfboard when he spots a dark hole. It is too late to react. With a blink of an eye, darkness falls all around him as he enters the storm drain.

For a moment, Rocky thinks, *I am spiraling upside down.*

No, I'm right side up.

Umm… Maybe not! Which way is up?

Okay. I think I am spinning out of control, Rocky exclaims to himself.

Rocky continues to roll through the concrete storm drain. The storm drain constantly curves left and right as the water continues rushing down the mountain.

Finally, SWOOSH, SWASH, KAWASH, Rocky shoots out of the drain tube into a much wider creek. The exit of the concrete tube sits at least ten feet higher than the creek below, and the time he spends in the air is exhilarating!

Rocky is an Olympic champion as he flies through the air twirling on his acrobatic surfboard. He imagines taking the Gold Medal at the world Olympics for the 10-mile water slide event.

Rocky bows to the cameras as he heads for the

THE FIGHT FOR FANG!

finish line. *The sweet taste of victory!*

Yes! Rocky pauses. *I won the Gold Medal!* When Rocky bows down to accept his Gold Medal, he feels… THUMP! KAPOW!… on his noggin!

Suddenly, Rocky hits the water of the lower creek. The impact sends him under the water, and he loses his grip. *My hope depends on that surfboard Rocky thinks aloud.*

Rocky you bozo, your survival depends on that little board and now all might be lost.

Now this must surely be the end! Rocky thinks just before…

CHAPTER 7

THE ROCK

*R*ocky surfaces, while choking on water. He experiences confusion by the hard impact. The makeshift surfboard pops up out of the water and, "BOINK," it hits him again in the head. As much as this hurts, Rocky quickly reaches for the board and holds on tight.

The water begins to slow and Rocky pulls himself partially onto the board. He lies there for a moment, exhausted. The board feels safe and he knows he needs to rest. That is, until Rocky feels logs and rocks hitting his paws and legs hanging in the water.

OOOH! OOOW! OOOH! The pain hits his body like a jolt of electricity. The pain reminds him of the time he placed his finger in an electrical socket. Rocky's hair stood straight out for a week like the porcupine that lived up the way.

THE FIGHT FOR FANG!

Rocky senses he needs to pull up onto the board. So with all of his strength, he makes one last desperate attempt to pull himself all the way up. There, Rocky finally stands up, legs shaking. His body quivering, Rocky refuses to give in. He needs to push on. He needs to be strong. He needs to be "**THE ROCK!**"

He imagines he is THE ROCK, the meanest, toughest, most terrifying raccoon of the world.

THE ROCK thinks he should flex his muscles. He makes several strong arm gestures shifting from side to side showing every bodybuilding pose imaginable. There is no one tougher than THE ROCK.

Rocky "THE ROCK" regains his rhythm. Finally feeling good, he sees something strange…a new shape far down the creek. His heart beats faster and faster as the shape comes into focus. If a raccoon could sweat, this is surely one of those times.

Rocky leans forward trying to make out the dark shape. "What could it be?" he whispers.

At this point, he almost leans too far forward and nearly falls off the surfboard!

Rocky whispers to himself. "Okay, okay, okay. I am definitely not THE ROCK."

Then another thought occurs to him… *Hello, Rocky, this might just be the end.*

CHAPTER 8

A HORRIBLE THING

The shape looks strangely dark with large eyes flashing bright orange. As Rocky makes out more of the shape, he sees huge teeth that appear to be swallowing everything that draw near.

Panicking, Rocky now swings the surfboard to the left, then to the right. Rocky picks up speed when he throws the surfboard back to the left. He leaves a huge wake trailing behind him. The last whip gives Rocky just enough speed to slide off a tree branch. Breaching the water, he sails off into the air.

Remember, what goes up must come down. Rocky hits the bank with a thud. He crashes face-first into the muddy bank. The mud tastes horrible, but there's no time to waste if he wants to escape this hideous creature.

Without stopping Rocky begins to run from the creek and the horrible thing that eats all that comes near it.

Rocky spots a huge and cavernous building. *Yes there*, he thinks, *I can get out of the rain and hide from this horrible creature hunting me*.

KAABANG! Rocky hits a window running at full speed!

THE FIGHT FOR FANG!

The impact almost knocks the wind out of him. Rocky panics now and begins to claw at the window, thinking nothing must stop him.

Rocky keeps clawing until he realizes the mud from his paws only smears the window and there is no way into the building. He slowly turns and slides down the window with his back to the glass.

Rocky begins to cry. He feels scared and lonely. Most of all he misses his brother, sister and Ma. He keeps thinking about the stories his Ma told about all those uncles and cousins who went to the big city and never returned!

This makes him cry even harder.

After some time, he calms down and wipes his eyes and face. He thinks he can somehow make out the shape of the horrible thing that almost had him for breakfast.

There in the distance stands a large black culvert with iron grates. The grates prevent creek debris from entering into the drain. Above the opening sits two emergency flashers to warn motorists from running off the road and into the creek.

To Rocky's relief there is no hideous creature. He closes his eyes and instantly falls asleep.

THE GREAT ADVENTURES OF ROCKY RACCOON

THE FIGHT FOR FANG!

PART 3
THE BIG CITY

CHAPTER 9

IT'S MAGIC

*I*n his sleep, Rocky dreams of the good times with his brother and sister. He dreams of how the three kits sneak out at night and go to the backside of the nearby strip mall. In the back of the mall sits a movie theater. Hmmm, the leftover food from the movies always tastes scrumptious.

Rocky found the back door of the theater was starting to fall apart at the bottom. Rocky, to his amazement, discovered if they wiggled hard, a little raccoon could fit through the door and into the inside of the theater.

The inside of the theater is always magical!

THE FIGHT FOR FANG!

Roxy knows exactly where to find the best popcorn and candy. And Rexy designed a way to squeeze into the seat cushions. He showed them how to push the lower seat down far enough to make a cradle to sit in. AHHH… just like the perfect nook of a tree but with the coziest warm seat.

The three kits sit in the front of the theater and watch the big movie screen. They love to throw popcorn and candy into the air and catch it as it falls.

Eating the candy like this is always tricky. When they miss the candy thrown into the air, it lands with a clank on the floor. Much to their delight, the clanking sound really annoys people watching the movie. Adding to the raccoons' excitement, the moviegoers can't see anyone throwing the candy since the kits are so small.

This often ends with the usher coming to look for the noisemakers. The three kits hide under the seats to escape the usher. This is also fun because people shriek and jump as the three kits move about under the seats.

Rocky, in particular, finds the movies always so fascinating. The movies have huge animals that talk and machines that travel into space. He even sees other creatures in the movies that can't possibly be real.

At this point in his dream, Rocky imagines how it feels to be on one of those rocket machines from the movies and how loud the engines sound.

THE GREAT ADVENTURES OF ROCKY RACCOON

In fact the engines are so, so, so very loud!

In fact, they are so loud Rocky cannot hear!

Rocky tries to yell for Roxy and Rexy in his dream… when without warning one of the rockets begins to take off.

Rocky holds tight to the rocket. Still not knowing what to do, he watches his sister and brother disappear as he leaves the ground.

"No, no, I can't lose you again," Rocky, screams. The noise from the space machine is deafening. Rocky keeps screaming out as he disappears into the sky, "No, don't go away!"

Rocky keeps thinking, *Just let go! Just let go! It's better to let go than not to be able to breathe.*

"BREATHE ROCKY."

CHAPTER 10

RETREAT!

Rocky wakes instantly. He shakes with fear when he opens his eyes and sees the blazing open end of a leaf blower.

The black tube of the blower points straight into his face. The noise of the engine is as loud as the rocket machine. The man holding the blower yells something and shakes the blower at him. From the man's gestures, he understands wild flailing arms are not a good thing.

With the speed of a mountain cat, and the agility of a Texas rattlesnake, Rocky runs from the man's attack. He runs along the sidewalk faster and faster until he spots the only living thing.

There between two buildings stands a large tree with ample shade and many places to hide among the branches.

To get to the tree, Rocky has to cross the biggest parking lot he has ever seen. He runs, leaping over curbs, shrubs, and running sprinklers. He dodges oncoming cars, and the porter emptying trashcans.

He scurries up the trunk of the tree and climbs into the highest branches. His heart pounds louder than he has ever heard it.

Now Rocky knows why no one ever returns from the Big City! No one ever returns to the quiet mountain that seemed so far away. Rocky curls up into a nook of the tree and settles in for a long, long sleep.

He sleeps undisturbed until late afternoon of the next day. In truth, he would still be sleeping if not for the commotion his stomach was making. Missing breakfast and dinner is certainly not a good thing. Rocky begins to squirm and stretch, feeling the bark scratch his coat. *Ahh, what a good feeling to scratch.* "Wow! Man, am I hungry!" he exclaims.

Rocky decides it's time to wake up and to begin finding his way home. His eyes are super crusty from crying the day before. Not to mention the mud from the creek smeared all over his face. The world looks oddly different through Rocky's half-open eyes. There are

THE FIGHT FOR FANG!

shadows everywhere. Along with those two big, luminous eyes staring back at him!

Rocky screams out, "AAAAGHHH!"

There on the tip of Rocky's nose sits a big frog. The frog clings on with both pads. The frog's head rests on Rocky's nose. "Hello, I thought you would never wake up," said the big frog.

"What is your name?" said the frog.

"I am Rocky and I am..." but before Rocky finishes his sentence, his stomach bellows a tremendous roar. Rocky smells something good and is unable to control his stomach. Before either can say another word, Rocky leaps toward the branches below. Branch after branch, Rocky bounds and swings, and then he appears to fly.

The young frog does not have a chance to jump aside when Rocky suddenly takes off. So he holds on tight to the end of Rocky's nose. At some point, Rocky's newfound friend manages to swing on top of Rocky's head. The frog, now a bronco-rider, holds onto Rocky's ears like a makeshift rope harness.

The ground begins approaching very fast. *Possibly the ground might be coming a little too fast*, thinks the frog. He thinks for sure that they will simply splat on the hard, bone breaking ground below.

But, within inches of the ground, Rocky leaps horizontally and now the two are off running across a section of the building. The whole time, the frog flops up and down like a bad toupee.

At this point, the frog figures if he sticks his rear legs into Rocky's ears, squeezing tightly, he can hold on better. However, Rocky does not like having anything in his ears and this only makes Rocky shake his head wildly.

The wild shaking becomes very unsafe for his young bronco-riding friend.

THE FIGHT FOR FANG!

CHAPTER 11

WALLY'S HAMBURGERS

*W*ith a final jump, Rocky lands on the top of a brightly colored yellow VW bug. The bubbletop car stops at the drive-thru window of Wally's hamburger joint.

Within a blink of an eye, the window opens and the Wally's employee hands a sack of food to the driver. Rocky can't contain himself and reaches over the edge of the roof. He snatches the top container of French fries and a hamburger from the open sack.

The driver lets out a hysterical **screech** and flings the bag of food into the air. Milk shakes, hamburgers, ketchup, mustard, and fries splatter all over the passengers in the car. Stunned and horrified by the sudden attack, the driver punches the gas pedal.

The car speeds off, leaving the Wally's employee halfway out the window trying to catch his balance. He looks like a crazy person, swinging arms wildly as he tries to catch himself before falling out the window. Rocky and his new bronco-riding friend lean over the front of the roof curiously watching the insanity within the car.

The woman driving the car realizes there are two very strange creatures staring at her upside down. She screams even more wildly while turning the car back and forth. The driver attempts to avoid hitting the two new passengers despite the fact they are stuck to the windshield!

The VW swerves through traffic and speeds along the sidewalk. Then the car crosses the road and heads back over into the next lane. Rocky and his bronco-riding friend try desperately to hang on. They keep scrambling from side to side.

Then suddenly Rocky's new friend stretches out with all four legs and like a bungee cord, he suctions them to the roof. His super stretch holds them in place to the top of the car. The frog bellows out, "OOHYEAH WHAT YA GONNA DOO, UHUH UHUH!"

Rocky sticks to the top of the car making his head look bigger than his body. His cheeks blow back as the car speeds up and heads for the four-lane road.

All of the passengers' arms and legs fly in and out of the car windows. The kids scream hysterically.

Everyone on the street stops and stares as the car speeds by speckled with milk shakes, ketchup, and fries. It looks like a Hot Wheels car right out of the package!

THE FIGHT FOR FANG!

THE GREAT ADVENTURES OF ROCKY RACCOON

PART 4
DOOMED!

CHAPTER 12

MEET FANG & EVILA

The car suddenly veers to the right and off onto a stone covered road. The road leads through a set of eerie black gates with hideous creatures carved on top of them. The road turns darker as the trees begin to cover the road.

The tree frog becomes afraid and lets go of the top of the car. He covers Rocky's eyes as if to protect both of them from something bad. The car hits a stone wall, and the rear of the vehicle begins lurching up. The rear wheels leave the ground and the kids slide into the front seat.

THE FIGHT FOR FANG!

Their faces press against the windshield and they blow hot steam onto the glass. Rocky and the frog slide down over the windshield staring at the mashed faces inside.

The car drops back into place and the doors open like an emergency hatch. The passengers crawl out with streaming tears and panic-stricken cries. The driver is hysterical and cannot stay up on her feet. She runs backwards, stumbling with each step.

Rocky hears a man's voice yell out, "Get 'em Fang!"

The man is very tall and square-shouldered. Rocky thinks he resembles the bad guy in one of the movies he watched in the magical theater.

Rocky continuously pulls the frog's fingers apart to see the man. Rocky keeps fussing at the tree frog to let him see. Finally, he pulls the frog's pads completely from his face.

That is when he sees Fang...

THE GREAT ADVENTURES OF ROCKY RACCOON

THE FIGHT FOR FANG!

The meanest, darkest, most hideous dog ever!

Fang's teeth are yellow with black tips that shine like diamonds. Hanging from his jowls is a slick of drool that vaporizes into steam as it touches the ground.

In unison they yell, "*Yikes!*" Rocky knows he must make a run for it before Fang gets between them and the trees in the backyard. Rocky runs down the hood of the car and slides over a slick moss covered fallen statue. The frog was not about to be left behind, and he grabs onto Rocky once again.

Before they reach the ground, Fang sprints towards them. An all-out test of speed, Rocky knows he must not lose. Fang closes in on them, and the tree frog fears *NOW, this must certainly be the end.*

Just as they reach the backyard, Rocky and his sidekick stumble across the edge of a pool. Rocky manages to change directions. Almost instantly, Fang lunges for them, missing them by only the smallest bit.

Not as agile Fang falls straight into the pool, causing a huge splash. Fang's lack of ability to swim amuses Rocky. The tree frog stands up on his two hind legs and gyrates, yelling, "OOHYEAH WHAT YA GONNA DOO, UHUH UHUH!"

Before Buff has the chance to repeat it twice, Rocky hears a loud growling from behind. "If Fang is in front of us then, who is behind us?" Rocky whispers. Slowly the two turn to see Fang's sister, Evila.

Evila corners them. Rocky spies an opening beneath the garden wall and takes the chance they will fit. Fang continues splashing in the pool. Rocky knows *I will make it to the trees if we can just get to the other side of the garden wall*.

Rocky bolts for the opening with Evila on their heels. Rocky runs headfirst into the opening. Oh no! His new friend is too big to fit through the opening at the same time as Rocky.

Rocky's new friend knocks backwards, only to be face to face with Evila.

The frog falls all the way off Rocky's back. Well, almost all the way off. A frog's tongue can be amazingly long and sticky when needed. At the last minute, the mighty frog spins, doing a full twist and snatches Rocky's tail with his tongue. The frog pops out just before Evila snaps down with her razor sharp teeth… just like a rubber band firing from a finger.

THE FIGHT FOR FANG!

Rocky runs with the intensity he did not think possible. His friend holds tightly to Rocky's tail. The frog begins running in the air to keep himself balanced. At times, he uses his hind legs to propel himself further into the air to avoid hitting the ground… and Evila's sharp teeth!

Rocky continuously looks back to be sure that his little friend is still holding tight. Rocky knows in his heart that, even if it means fighting Fang and Evila, he will stop if his new friend falls.

Rocky will not leave his new friend alone.

Once again, Evila gains ground on them. After Rocky makes his escape through the wall, Evila circles and leaps over the wall in pursuit.

Fang also recovers from his splash in the pool. He closes in on them from the opposite side. If these two friends do not reach the woods in time, they'll be goners.

CHAPTER 14

UNCLE PAULIE

$\mathcal{M}$eanwhile, no one witnesses the strange commotion overhead in the trees. The tree canopy begins to thicken. Very little light penetrates below the branches.

There within the darkness hide many pairs of red glowing eyes following the action that is taking place below them. Then in a flash a thunderous wave of debris comes hurtling down onto Fang and Evila. Nuts, berries, seeds, branches, stones, bones, and anything that can be thrown. At one point, a full can of pork and beans comes crashing down.

Berry stains cover Fang and Evila and they begin to feel the sting of sharp objects. A large branch hits Fang on the snout and slams him headfirst into a pile of thorn bushes. He yelps loudly and turns to run for cover.

Bewildered, Evila follows Fang.

"How can anything defeat the mighty Fang?" Evila whispers.

She continues to whisper this as they retreat to the safety of the yard. Evila keeps shouting at Fang to return and fight.

Fang responds, "Not this time, Sis. There will be a time for each rascal to show themself and then I will get my revenge." And with a large howl, he tells those who defeated him today that victory will be mine someday. With the acceptance of his defeat, Fang lets out a menacing howl once again. In the most horrifying and scary voice Rocky has ever heard, he makes out what Fang said.

"You will be my lunch tomorrow."

At this point, Rocky stops and looks about to understand why the dogs retreated. What he sees astonishes him! Dozens of raccoons stand tall in front of him and hang from the trees.

"Welcome my friends, I am Paulie. And who might you be?" asks the noblest and largest of the raccoons.

"I am Rocky and this is… ?"

Rocky realizes he has been most impolite by never

THE FIGHT FOR FANG!

asking the frog his name. Rocky finds it unusual that the frog continues to ride with him in all of this danger even though Rocky has been so unkind.

What an unusually good and loyal friend this frog must be to stay by my side, even though I know nothing about him!

CHAPTER 15

BUFFARINO

("BIG FROG")

*T*he frog responds, "I am Buffarino, or, you can call me Buff." The overly large frog now takes charge.

Several of the raccoons come forward from the forest with different musical instruments. They play for the newcomers welcoming them to their home.

They present a set of makeshift bongos made from roots covered with canvas. They also pull out different types of flutes made from reeds. To top it all off, they have a tattered old violin the raccoons saved from the trash. They use it as a bass.

The raccoons all start singing and playing, "Buffarino, Buff, Buff, Bufareeenoooo." Buff jumps in and

THE FIGHT FOR FANG!

begins playing the bongos. The crowd goes wild, and Rocky starts to enjoy the shenanigans. Just as the group readies to finish the song, Buff launches into a solo on the bongos. As a finale, Buff hits the drums one last time and leaps over the drums landing on his rear legs. Buff's arms stretch out, and in a low tenor voice, he shouts, "Buffarino!"

Paulie grabs Rocky and quietly says, "Follow me." Off they go leaving Buffarino behind to entertain the crowd of raccoons.

As they walk through the forest, Paulie politely asks Rocky if his mother might not be the chattiest of all raccoons. "Why yes!" Rocky exclaims, "how did you guess?"

"She is my sister and I used to play with you before I left for the Big City." Paulie hesitates for a moment and then asks, "Do they still call her Chatty Cathy?" They both chuckle for some time.

They continue walking through the forest to an opening in a large stone wall. On the other side of the stone wall appear rolling hills filled with grapevines... the largest vineyard in Texas. Rocky's stomach talks to him, and he starts to lick his lips. Rocky exclaims, "Uncle Paulie, how incredibly fantastic."

Uncle Paulie explains to him that the owners of the vineyard make wine. He found the vineyard when it was just starting, and could not bring himself to leave. Over many months, Uncle Paulie invited friends to come live in the forest, and to help with the harvesting of the grapes for their own delight.

Uncle Paulie thought the owners would not mind a few grapes missing from time to time. But as time went by, too many raccoons began to show up. The parties were fun, but now there was trouble. The owners brought

THE FIGHT FOR FANG!

Fang and Evila to protect the vineyard from the overly hungry raccoons.

Rocky remembered what Fang said, "There will be a time for each rascal to show themself and then, I will get my revenge."

Uncle Paulie continues with Fang's words. "You will be my lunch tomorrow."

CHAPTER 16

LUNCH MENU

*R*ocky finds Buff back at the party and tells him what he had seen. Buff suggests they take a tour of the vineyard tomorrow to see if they can help his Uncle Paulie.

All of the raccoons settle into the trees for the night, each finding a comfortable nook. Sunrise fast approaches and they all look forward to a good day's sleep.

The morning arrives with Fang howling ferociously. In an instant, all of the raccoons slide further up into the darkness of the trees. It looks as though they never move a muscle. Buff stares across the trees as they lift magically higher into the canopy.

Rocky hears Fang and Evila wandering down below.

THE FIGHT FOR FANG!

They sniff every inch of the forest floor to find a way to get to the raccoons.

Neither Rocky nor Buff wants to get up. Buff mumbles as he stretches out over Rocky's eyes. He thinks he can act as a blindfold and after all Rocky is super warm. Buff shouts down, "Don't you two bozos realize that raccoons are nocturnal?" Rocky reminds Buff that he is in fact nocturnal as well!

For the rest of the day they hear the shuffle of Fang and Evila moving about the forest.

Uncle Paulie wakes Rocky and Buff around five in the evening. "If you want to see the vineyard, come with me." Rocky has to peel off his blindfold…Buff, for he too still sleeps soundly.

The two friends move slowly at first, and then gradually give into Uncle Paulie's request. The three bandits move very carefully to see to it that not a one of them will be on today's lunch menu.

Uncle Paulie, Rocky and Buff move quickly through the forest, checking each hideout for the evil duo, Fang and Evila. Interestingly enough they find no sign of the gruesome twosome. Uncle Paulie warns Rocky and Buff to be extremely careful. "I figure they are having dinner, and probably settling down for the night. There should be no trouble tonight," Rocky states.

They reach the gate in the stone wall leading into the vineyard. There on top of the gates hover the same scary figurines that Rocky saw the day before at the house. Sitting on Rocky's head, Buff whispers, "Don't be afraid, they are only statues." With that, Rocky slows down and looks up.

A long slick of drool lands on Buff, then slides onto Rocky's nose. The eyes of the statues turn crimson red. They both yell together, "It's Fang and Evila!"

THE FIGHT FOR FANG!

THE GREAT ADVENTURES OF ROCKY RACCOON

THE FIGHT FOR FANG!

PART 5
KEEP YOUR WITS!

CHAPTER 17

THE LAUGHING SCENE

Fang leaps from the stone wall with his mouth wide open. Fang's eyes burn like lasers. Rocky thinks, *This must certainly be the end!*

Fantastically, Buff leaps from Rocky's back and grabs Fang's tongue. Buff swings under Fang's body and pulls the tongue as far back as he can. Buff yells, "Oohya, huhuh, you're never goin' to stop me!" He lets go of the stretched tongue. Fang's tongue snaps back so hard that it makes his head bob up and down like a bobble head.

Then without warning, Fang feels a sudden **smack** on the belly. Slowly growling Fang lowers his head, and looks under his body. There holding tight to his belly is Buff, who slyly says, "Hello." He begins tickling Fang with

THE FIGHT FOR FANG!

his large pads and fingers.

Fang rolls over and starts laughing hysterically. "Stop, Stop, Stop! No, No! I can't take it!" he howls. Relentless, Buff puts Fang into hysterics.

Evila leaps from her perch and attempts to rescue Fang. Fang laughs so hard that Evila is unable to help. She keeps shouting at Fang, "Get up, get up, Fang, and fight them." But Fang cannot stop laughing.

With one last attempt, Evila snorts at Fang, "Get up. No one defeats the mighty Fang."

However, Evila did not notice Buff leaping from Fang towards the ground beneath her. Then suddenly, Evila feels a **smack** on her belly! Evila's eyes begin to light up, and glow as bright as a street-light.

Then Buff hits with all his strength, and begins tickling Evila. She too drops to the ground and rolls over with laughter. Evila wriggles and rolls, laughing and crying. It is the craziest sight!

Fang rolls over onto his stomach exhausted. He watches Evila squirm and laugh. "Kinda fun huh, Sis!" Fang says.

"I will do anything you ask just stop, please stop, stop, stop!" Evila laughs and shouts.

Buff stops tickling Evila, and jumps back onto Rocky.

Evila rolls over still laughing, tears streaming down her face and nose.

Rocky repeats Evila's words, "You will do anything?"

Both Evila and Fang speak at the same time, "Yes, we will do anything."

With this announcement, Rocky has an idea.

CHAPTER 18

A FULL HOUSE

*R*ocky stretches out in front of Evila and Fang to explain his plan. Buff and Uncle Paulie join them. They feel excited that they have won the fight against the evil duo without a single scratch.

Rocky knows if Uncle Paulie and the others understood which grapes are for harvesting, and which are not, there might be a solution. He also thinks there might be other goodies to be had. The restaurant located in the vineyard, might have some delicious left over food to throw out.

Rocky suggests they strike a deal. The raccoons harvest the grapes under Evila's and Fang's directions.

The raccoons can easily harvest the grapes and load them into baskets.

In return, the owners might reward Evila and Fang for protecting the vineyard. Then if there are any extras, Fang and Evila will see to it that the raccoons are well fed.

Uncle Paulie wants to feel he is adding something to this negotiation. So he offers, "I will also promise to keep the vineyard free of mice and rats. You know how they can often escape because they are so small."

Rocky winks at Fang in a gesture to say "play along."

Fang responds by saying, "Those smaller ones are hard to catch."

Suddenly, in the dark they hear a shrill shrieEEEEk! The sound comes from the stone wall above them. There in the dark stands a small mouse. The mouse remains rigid with eyes as big as the moon. Without another sound, he scurries away!

This camaraderie makes Uncle Paulie feel there

needs to be some good old card playing to seal the deal. Uncle Paulie pulls out a deck of cards from what appears to be nowhere and challenges the others to a game.

Fang states, "I think there is a Full House in the cards tonight."

All of the new friends chuckle as they start the night's play.

CHAPTER 19

REUNION STATION

Paulie spends the next few days speaking with each raccoon in the forest. He needs to be sure they all agree to stick to the rules. They also have to take orders from Fang and Evila. There shall be no deserters. Even if only one raccoon steps out of line, everyone will lose.

One evening, Uncle Paulie covers each raccoon nest. He is about to turn in for the night, when he sees a stranger standing in the dim light. The stranger has unusual bandit marks, and looks as though he is part of a warrior tribe. As the stranger nears, the moon casts an eerie glow across his face. Uncle Paulie becomes quite afraid.

However, as the stranger comes closer Uncle

THE FIGHT FOR FANG!

Paulie's fears subside. Uncle Paulie smiles with relief, and places his arm around the stranger. "Come with me, old friend."

The next afternoon Uncle Paulie and the others arrive at the stone gates as promised. There are dozens of raccoons, each with helmets made of twigs and straw. The raccoons take their job very seriously. They form lines like soldiers and follow Uncle Paulie into the vineyard. Then they part into lines like band members at a football game. Each line moves into a different row of grapes.

The lines of raccoons follow orders from the former evil duo, Fang and Evila, and they all begin to move into position. With Fang standing on the hill looking over the vineyard, he lets out a terrifying howl. On cue, every raccoon removes his or her helmet. Fang laughs aloud. So loud in fact, the entire vineyard stands still for a moment. Fang laughs again, and says to Evila, "Look, the helmets are baskets!"

Rocky feels good about his idea after seeing how well things are going.

Again, Buff stretches out with all fours on top of Rocky's head. In this moment of silence, Buff whispers to Rocky, "Who is that band of strangers coming up the path with your Uncle Paulie?"

Rocky sits up straighter as he views the small band of raccoons approaching. The sun shines brightly behind the strangers making it difficult for Rocky to see them.

Rocky keeps squinting trying to make out the strangers' faces. Rocky reaches up, and rubs his eyes. He still cannot see any better.

Then Buff shouts, "Here, let me help," covering Rocky's eyes with his fingers. Rocky becomes frantic and desperately tries to pull Buff's sticky fingers apart. But before he manages it, he feels a body pounce on him. They all fall backwards.

Shocked Rocky sees it is Roxy!

Rocky remains stunned, *How could this be?* And Rexy! *Where, did they come from? How did they find me?* "I can't believe it!" Rocky shouts.

Then Rocky goes silent for a moment. Standing next to Uncle Paulie is Ma. Rocky runs to her, and wraps his arms around her. He gives her the biggest, mushiest hug ever.

Rocky thinks, *Now, this is the bestest night of all time!*

THE FIGHT FOR FANG!

CHAPTER 20

THE END

*M*a squeezes the air out of Rocky. She hugs him so hard that he decides to wiggle free from her grasp. It's no use, she has him in a raccoon hug and he just hangs there like the stuffed dolls he has seen the young girls carrying at picnics. Finally, Rocky whispers, "Ma, now you know why no one ever returns home from the Big City." With that, she releases Rocky from her grip and starts to laugh and cry at the same time.

Buff, his traveling companion and new best friend, looks on with admiration and thinks to himself,

NOW! Surely this must NOT be the end!

THE GREAT ADVENTURES OF ROCKY RACCOON

EPILOGUE

IS IT THE END?

Rocky and Buff settle down for the morning after spending the last month or so watching after the operations at the vineyard. Harvesting sure can be hard work but Rocky feels good about the compromise they made with Fang and Evila.

Other than the weather, the last week has gone well. However, the rain keeps getting worse over the last few days until finally the paths in the vineyard are sloppy, muddy, and virtually non-passable.

There was so much water this morning that at one point Buff grabs a helmet from a worker and throws it into the path upside down. Within seconds, Rocky's friend jumps in the helmet, nose peering over the edge, eyes as large as the grapes they pick, and he sails down the path like a bobsled. Buff hangs on, screaming like a banshee, and spinning like a top. Down the vineyard, he sails. Laughing and laughing as he spins and twirls. No one tries to stop him. They all know he is heading for a fate worse than he has ever met.

There at the end of the path lies a large fenced yard with the biggest pile of cow pies ever! The pile is so tall that it takes a tractor to lift the next batch to the top.

Guess where Buff is heading!

Before, Buff realizes his predicament, the torrent of water picks up speed. Buff stops screaming and looks in sheer horror as he notices the fence approaching. He ducks just "in the nick of time" before getting his head chopped off by the fence rail.

Ohh, then there's still the other matter of landing in a big old stinky, sloppy wet, pile of cow pies! Buff quickly shoots out his tongue to grab the fence rail and pull himself to safety. The wood's slippery wet surface forces his tongue to slide off the rail leaving him suspended in the air. Buff looks temporarily caught by some unseen hand. Then suddenly, Sph...latt his body hurls straight into the pile of cow pies.

Those with the best view begin to laugh hysterically as Buff pulls himself up out of the pile of OOOOZE.

THE FIGHT FOR FANG!

Rocky goes to Buff's rescue and holding his own nose, he picks his friend up out of the unmentionable smelly stuff. "Sorry Buff, I have no choice but to dip you, my best friend, into this torrent of water." *The torrent of water coming down the path will hopefully cleanse you of this awful stink!*

"Besides, Buff there's no possible way I will let you ride bronco-style back to the safety of the camp smelling like a cow pie." So the two wade through the water back to the canopy of the trees and settle in for the morning.

The rain begins to hit harder and harder in the midday. Exhausted, Rocky simply pulls down a few branches for more cover and tries to pretend to be in Hawaii again. He wants to be somewhere warm and dry.

Rocky imagines being back on his surfboard and riding the waves on the North Shore. The water rolls over him and he shivers with the cold wet feeling. He targets what appears to be one of the largest waves ever and the urge comes over him to try to ride it. He knows he can ride the tube all the way back into shore. He just knows he can do it.

Rocky expertly cuts back and forth on the wall of the wave.

The wave keeps getting bigger and bigger. He struggles to keep on top of the surfboard. He knows to keep the board from running too far up the wave. If he runs too far up the wave's wall, it will lead to toppling over into the smashing, grinding water in the trough. Rocky realizes suddenly this was not one of the bestest of ideas. He hangs on tighter to the sides of the surfboard as he fights to stay on it.

Suddenly the board shoots straight up the wave and throws Rocky backwards into the frothy water. The water pulls him to the bottom of the ocean.

Rocky gasps for air just before he lands in the water. Rocky feels the back of his head hit the surface hard and knocks the air out from his chest. Rocky struggles in an effort to find the surface of the water. Suddenly, in a burst of frantic fighting he wakes up from the dream.

Rocky fights with a tarp tied down to the sides of a large truck. Between Rocky and the tarp hangs Buff -- trying hard not to be hit by Rocky as he swings at the tarp to get free.

Rocky relaxes when he figures out that he is not drowning in the biggest wave he has ever seen. Rocky stops swinging wildly. With relief, Buff drops from the tarp and falls onto Rocky.

"Rocky, where are we?" whispers Buff.

"What are we going to do?" whispers Rocky.

STORY TELLER'S NOTES

The story of Rocky Raccoon began as a nightly tale. Cameron and I would recap the previous evening of Rocky's adventures before adding to Rocky's new challenges. The tales behind The Great Adventures of Rocky Raccoon express to young and old that it is okay to grow up away from the influences of Ma and Pa and that life is your personal magical adventure filled with fun and mystery.

The process took almost 8 months to develop the first story. Along the way, there were moments the tale appeared to be at an end and Rocky would not go on. At which point I would add "this must be the end" or "This must certainly be the end!" or some derivative of my statement. I really was hoping we had reached **The End!**

Cameron insisted **it was not The End!**

THE FIGHT FOR FANG!

What I did not realize is how positively Cameron sees the world. In Cameron's mind, there will always be a chance to overcome the challenges presented in this world. Children show us just how simple it can be to press the forward button and continue!

Yes, we can learn from Rocky and Buff in their special magical way to step back from a situation and exclaim, "***This surely must not be the end!***"

I also discovered the bond of loyalty we form between our children, friends and family through Rocky's story. I grew to enjoy Cameron's process of teaching me all that I forget about life with each new Rocky adventure. Unfortunately, the process did end with the printing of a handful of copies and a personal visit to Cameron's classroom to read aloud the book.

That is surely the end. I thought!

The story sat on the shelf for a few years until one day I found the last copy. Cameron and I began reading with wonderment. *"Did we really write this story?"* we asked ourselves. With the encouragement of Cameron's teacher and his mother, we took on a tremendous endeavor to edit, illustrate, and publish the first tale in the series, The Great Adventures of Rocky Raccoon. The Fight for Fang, the first in the series, presents Rocky with the challenge of vanquishing a foe without harm.

Cameron and I are grateful to Katherine Friend, Claudia Hausken and Jonathan Tyner for their efforts to correct our use of grammar.

THE GREAT ADVENTURES OF ROCKY RACCOON

A great many kudos need to go out to Jeanine Henning for her imaginative drawings. Relief came from Darren Rozier, Guardian Prepress & Production for formatting the digital and print copies.

We owe our good fortune to the staff at McCarthy Print, Inc. for handling the offset and digital press. Their guidance and support is invaluable.

Ahh, yes, a multitude of "high fives" goes out to Mrs. Wells and Mrs. Fry for encouraging Cameron to express his creativity in writing and storytelling.

We would also like to thank our family, grandparents, and staff at Zinger for affording us the time to finish this project.

Mahalo Nui Loa!

THE FIGHT FOR FANG!

ROCKY WILL SEE YOU RIDING THE WAVES IN HAWAII

OR SHALL IT BE ...

WRESTLING WITH THE 'GATORS IN NEW ORLEANS!

CAST YOUR VOTE FOR ROCKY'S NEXT GREAT ADVENTURE AT

WWW.ROCKYRACCOONKIDS.COM

Cameron and Michael Ferweda are a dynamic son and father authorship team who love to tell stories. The imagination of these two storytellers is vastly different in style, by a mere 40 years. Yet, the blending of each of their stories turns into a thrilling read. A 5th grader, Cameron is the brains behind the book. Both Cameron and Michael are growing up and old in Austin, Texas. Visit us each and every weekend in person at Zinger Hardware, or at the following sites:

www.rockyraccoonkids.com
www.zingerhardware.com

Cameron & Michael

ADVENTURE...   LAUGHTER...   DOOM!